Sappho: One Hundred Lyrics

Bliss Carman

Contents

SAPPHO: ONE HUNDRED LYRICS

BY

Bliss Carman

INTRODUCTION

THE POETRY OF SAPPHO.--If all the poets and all the lovers of poetry should be asked to name the most precious of the priceless things which time has wrung in tribute from the triumphs of human genius, the answer which would rush to every tongue would be "The Lost Poems of Sappho." These we know to have been jewels of a radiance so imperishable that the broken gleams of them still dazzle men's eyes, whether shining from the two small brilliants and the handful of star-dust which alone remain to us, or reflected merely from the adoration of those poets of old time who were so fortunate as to witness their full glory.

For about two thousand five hundred years Sappho has held her place as not only the supreme poet of her sex, but the chief lyrist of all lyrists. Every one who reads acknowledges her fame, concedes her supremacy; but to all except poets and Hellenists her name is a vague and uncomprehended splendour, rising secure above a persistent mist of misconception. In spite of all that is in these days being written about Sappho, it is perhaps not out of place now to inquire, in a few words, into the substance of this supremacy which towers so unassailably secure from what appear to be such shadowy foundations.

First, we have the witness of her contemporaries. Sappho was at the height of her career about six centuries before Christ, at a period when lyric poetry was peculiarly esteemed and cultivated at the centres of Greek life. Among the *Molic* peoples of the Isles, in particular, it had been carried to a high pitch of perfection, and its forms had become the subject of assiduous study. Its technique was exact, complex, extremely elaborate, minutely regulated; yet the essential fires of sincerity, spontaneity, imagination and passion were flaming with undiminished heat behind the fixed forms and restricted measures. The very metropolis of this lyric realm was Mitylene of Lesbos, where, amid the myrtle groves and temples, the sunlit silver of the fountains, the hyacinth gardens by a soft blue sea, Beauty and Love in their young warmth could fuse the most rigid forms to fluency. Here Sappho was the acknowledged queen of song--revered, studied, imitated, served, adored by a little court of attendants and disciples, loved and hymned by Alcaeus, and acclaimed by her fellow craftsmen throughout Greece as the wonder of her age. That all the tributes of her contemporaries show reverence not less for her personality than for her genius is sufficient answer to the calumnies with which the ribald jesters of that later period, the corrupt and shameless writers of Athenian comedy, strove to defile her fame. It is sufficient, also, to warrant our regarding the picturesque but scarcely dignified story of her vain pursuit of Phaon and her frenzied leap from the Cliff of Leucas as nothing more than a poetic myth, reminiscent, perhaps, of the myth of Aphrodite and Adonis--who is, indeed, called Phaon in some versions. The story is further discredited by the fact that we find no mention of it in Greek literature-- even among those Attic comedians who would have clutched at it so eagerly and given it so gross a turn--till a date more than two hundred years after Sappho's death. It is a myth which has begotten some exquisite literature, both in prose and verse, from Ovid's famous epistle to Addison's gracious fantasy and some impassioned and imperishable dithyrambs of Mr. Swinburne; but one need not accept the story as a fact in order to appreciate the beauties which flowered out from its coloured unreality.

The applause of contemporaries, however, is not always justified by the verdict of after-times, and does not always secure an immortality of renown. The fame of Sappho has a more stable basis. Her work was in the world's possession for not far short of a thousand years--a thousand years of changing tastes, searching criticism, and familiar use. It had to endure the wear and tear of quotation, the commonizing touch of the school and the market-place. And under this test its glory grew ever more and more conspicuous. Through those thousand years poets and critics vied with one another in proclaiming her verse the one unmatched exemplar of lyric art. Such testimony, even though not a single fragment remained to us from which to judge her poetry for ourselves, might well convince us that the supremacy acknowledged by those who knew all the triumphs of the genius of old Greece was beyond the assault of any modern rival. We might safely accept the sustained judgment of a thousand years of Greece.

Fortunately for us, however, two small but incomparable odes and a few scintillating fragments have survived, quoted and handed down in the eulogies of critics and expositors. In these the wisest minds, the greatest poets, and the most inspired teachers of modern days have found justification for the unanimous verdict of antiquity. The tributes of Addison, Tennyson, and others, the throbbing paraphrases and ecstatic interpretations of Swinburne, are too well known to call for special comment in this brief note; but the concise summing up of her genius by Mr. Watts-Dunton in his remarkable essay on poetry is so convincing and illuminating that it seems to demand quotation here: "Never before these songs were sung, and never since did the human soul, in the grip of a fiery passion, utter a cry like hers; and, from the executive point of view, in directness, in lucidity, in that high, imperious verbal economy which only nature can teach the artist, she has no equal, and none worthy to take the place of second."

The poems of Sappho so mysteriously lost to us seem to have consisted of at least nine books of odes, together with *epithalamia*, epigrams, elegies, and monodies. Of the several theories which have been advanced to account for their disappearance, the most plausible seems to be that which represents them as having been burned at Byzantium in the year 380 Anno Domini, by command of Gregory Nazianzen, in order that his own poems might be studied in their stead and the morals of the people thereby improved. Of the efficacy of this act no means of judging has come down to us.

In recent years there has arisen a great body of literature upon the subject of Sappho, most of it the abstruse work of scholars writing for scholars. But the gist of it all, together with the minutest surviving fragment of her verse, has been made available to the general reader in English by Mr. Henry T. Wharton, in whose altogether admirable little volume we find all that is known and the most apposite of all that has been said up to the present day about

"Love's priestess, mad with pain and joy of song,
Song's priestess, mad with joy and pain of love."

Perhaps the most perilous and the most alluring venture in the whole field of poetry is that which Mr. Carman has undertaken in attempting to give us in English verse those lost poems of Sappho of which fragments have survived. The task is obviously not one of translation or of paraphrasing, but of imaginative and, at the same time, interpretive construction. It is as if a sculptor of to-day were to set himself, with reverence, and trained craftsmanship, and studious familiarity with the spirit, technique, and atmosphere of his subject, to restore some statues of Polyclitus or Praxiteles of which he had but a broken arm, a foot, a knee, a finger upon which to build. Mr. Carman's method, apparently, has been to imagine each lost lyric as discovered, and then to translate it; for the indefinable flavour of the translation is maintained throughout, though accompanied by the fluidity and freedom of purely original work.

C.G.D. ROBERTS.

Now to please my little friend
I must make these notes of spring,
With the soft south-west wind in them
And the marsh notes of the frogs.

I must take a gold-bound pipe,
And outmatch the bubbling call
From the beechwoods in the sunlight,
From the meadows in the rain.

SAPPHO

I

Cyprus, Paphos, or Panormus
May detain thee with their splendour
Of oblations on thine altars,
O imperial Aphrodite.

Yet do thou regard, with pity   5
For a nameless child of passion,
This small unfrequented valley
By the sea, O sea-born mother.

II

What shall we do, Cytherea?
Lovely Adonis is dying.
  Ah, but we mourn him!

Will he return when the Autumn
Purples the earth, and the sunlight 5
  Sleeps in the vineyard?

Will he return when the Winter
Huddles the sheep, and Orion
  Goes to his hunting?

Ah, but thy beauty, Adonis, 10
With the soft spring and the south wind,
  Love and desire!

III

Power and beauty and knowledge,--
Pan, Aphrodite, or Hermes,--
Whom shall we life-loving mortals
  Serve and be happy?

Lo now, your garlanded altars,   5
Are they not goodly with flowers?
Have ye not honour and pleasure
  In lovely Lesbos?

Will ye not, therefore, a little
Hearten, impel, and inspire 10
One who adores, with a favour
  Threefold in wonder?

IV

O Pan of the evergreen forest,
Protector of herds in the meadows,
Helper of men at their toiling,--
Tillage and harvest and herding,--
How many times to frail mortals   5
  Hast thou not hearkened!

Now even I come before thee
With oil and honey and wheat-bread,
Praying for strength and fulfilment
Of human longing, with purpose   10
Ever to keep thy great worship
  Pure and undarkened.

            *   *   *   *   *

O Hermes, master of knowledge,
Measure and number and rhythm,
Worker of wonders in metal,   15
Moulder of malleable music,
So often the giver of secret
  Learning to mortals!

Now even I, a fond woman,
Frail and of small understanding,   20
Yet with unslakable yearning
Greatly desiring wisdom,

Come to the threshold of reason
  And the bright portals.

        *   *   *   *   *

And thou, sea-born Aphrodite,   25
In whose beneficent keeping
Earth, with her infinite beauty,
Colour and fashion and fragrance,
Glows like a flower with fervour
  Where woods are vernal!   30

Touch with thy lips and enkindle
This moon-white delicate body,
Drench with the dew of enchantment
This mortal one, that I also
Grow to the measure of beauty   35
  Fleet yet eternal.

V

O Aphrodite,
God-born and deathless,
Break not my spirit
With bitter anguish:
Thou wilful empress, 5
I pray thee, hither!

As once aforetime

Well thou didst hearken
To my voice far off,--
Listen, and leaving   10
Thy father's golden
House in yoked chariot,

Come, thy fleet sparrows
Beating the mid-air
Over the dark earth. 15
Suddenly near me,
Smiling, immortal,
Thy bright regard asked

What had befallen,--
Why I had called thee,--   20
What my mad heart then
Most was desiring.
"What fair thing wouldst thou
Lure now to love thee?

"Who wrongs thee, Sappho? 25
If now she flies thee,
Soon shall she follow;--
Scorning thy gifts now,
Soon be the giver;--
And a loth loved one 30

"Soon be the lover."
So even now, too,
Come and release me
From mordant love pain,
And all my heart's will   35
Help me accomplish!

VI

Peer of the gods he seems,
Who in thy presence
Sits and hears close to him
Thy silver speech-tones
And lovely laughter. 5

Ah, but the heart flutters
Under my bosom,
When I behold thee
Even a moment;
Utterance leaves me; 10

My tongue is useless;
A subtle fire
Runs through my body;
My eyes are sightless,
And my ears ringing; 15

I flush with fever,
And a strong trembling
Lays hold upon me;
Paler than grass am I,
Half dead for madness.   20

Yet must I, greatly
Daring, adore thee,

As the adventurous
Sailor makes seaward
For the lost sky-line 25

And undiscovered
Fabulous islands,
Drawn by the lure of
Beauty and summer
And the sea's secret. 30

VII

The Cyprian came to thy cradle,
When thou wast little and small,
And said to the nurse who rocked thee
"Fear not thou for the child:

"She shall be kindly favoured,   5
And fair and fashioned well,
As befits the Lesbian maidens
And those who are fated to love."

Hermes came to thy cradle,
Resourceful, sagacious, serene,   10
And said, "The girl must have knowledge,
To lend her freedom and poise.

Naught will avail her beauty,
If she have not wit beside.

She shall be Hermes' daughter,   15
Passing wise in her day."

Great Pan came to thy cradle,
With calm of the deepest hills,
And smiled, "They have forgotten
The veriest power of life.   20

"To kindle her shapely beauty,
And illumine her mind withal,
I give to the little person
The glowing and craving soul."

VIII

Aphrodite of the foam,
Who hast given all good gifts,
And made Sappho at thy will
Love so greatly and so much,

Ah, how comes it my frail heart   5
Is so fond of all things fair,
I can never choose between
Gorgo and Andromeda?

IX

Nay, but always and forever
Like the bending yellow grain,
Or quick water in a channel,
Is the heart of man.

Comes the unseen breath in power 5
Like a great wind from the sea,
And we bow before his coming,
Though we know not why.

X

Let there be garlands, Dica,
Around thy lovely hair.
And supple sprays of blossom
Twined by thy soft hands.

Whoso is crowned with flowers   5
Has favour with the gods,
Who have no kindly eyes
For the ungarlanded.

XI

When the Cretan maidens
Dancing up the full moon
Round some fair new altar,
Trample the soft blossoms of fine grass,

There is mirth among them. 5
Aphrodite's children
Ask her benediction
On their bridals in the summer night.

XII

In a dream I spoke with the Cyprus-born,
  And said to her,
"Mother of beauty, mother of joy,
Why hast thou given to men

"This thing called love, like the ache of a wound   5
  In beauty's, side,
To burn and throb and be quelled for an hour
And never wholly depart?"

And the daughter of Cyprus said to me,
  "Child of the earth, 10
Behold, all things are born and attain,
But only as they desire,---

"The sun that is strong, the gods that are wise,
  The loving heart,
Deeds and knowledge and beauty and joy,--   15
But before all else was desire."

XIII

Sleep thou in the bosom
Of the tender comrade,
While the living water
Whispers in the well-run,
And the oleanders   5
Glimmer in the moonlight.

Soon, ah, soon the shy birds
Will be at their fluting,
And the morning planet
Rise above the garden;   10
For there is a measure
Set to all things mortal.

XIV

Hesperus, bringing together

All that the morning star scattered,--

Sheep to be folded in twilight,
Children for mothers to fondle,--

Me too will bring to the dearest,   5
Tenderest breast in all Lesbos.

XV

In the grey olive-grove a small brown bird
Had built her nest and waited for the spring.
But who could tell the happy thought that came
To lodge beneath my scarlet tunic's fold?

All day long now is the green earth renewed   5
With the bright sea-wind and the yellow blossoms.
From the cool shade I hear the silver plash
Of the blown fountain at the garden's end.

XVI

In the apple boughs the coolness
Murmurs, and the grey leaves flicker
Where sleep wanders.

In this garden all the hot noon
I await thy fluttering footfall5
Through the twilight.

XVII

Pale rose leaves have fallen
In the fountain water;
And soft reedy flute-notes
Pierce the sultry quiet.

But I wait and listen, 5
Till the trodden gravel
Tells me, all impatience,
It is Phaon's footstep.

XVIII

The courtyard of her house is wide
And cool and still when day departs.
Only the rustle of leaves is there
  And running water.

And then her mouth, more delicate 5

Than the frail wood-anemone,
Brushes my cheek, and deeper grow
  The purple shadows.

XIX

There is a medlar-tree
Growing in front of my lover's house,
  And there all day
The wind makes a pleasant sound.

And when the evening comes,   5
We sit there together in the dusk,
  And watch the stars
Appear in the quiet blue.

XX

I behold Arcturus going westward
Down the crowded slope of night-dark azure,
While the Scorpion with red Antares
Trails along the sea-line to the southward.

From the ilex grove there comes soft laughter,--   5
My companions at their glad love-making,--

While that curly-headed boy from Naxos
With his jade flute marks the purple quiet.

XXI

Softly the first step of twilight
Falls on the darkening dial,
One by one kindle the lights
    In Mitylene.

Noises are hushed in the courtyard, 5
The busy day is departing,
Children are called from their games,--
    Herds from their grazing.

And from the deep-shadowed angles
Comes the soft murmur of lovers,   10
Then through the quiet of dusk
    Bright sudden laughter.

From the hushed street, through the portal,
Where soon my lover will enter,
Comes the pure strain of a flute   15
    Tender with passion.

XXII

Once you lay upon my bosom,
While the long blue-silver moonlight
Walked the plain, with that pure passion
  All your own.

Now the moon is gone, the Pleiads 5
Gone, the dead of night is going;
Slips the hour, and on my bed
  I lie alone.

XXIII

I loved thee, Atthis, in the long ago,
When the great oleanders were in flower
In the broad herded meadows full of sun.
And we would often at the fall of dusk
Wander together by the silver stream,   5
When the soft grass-heads were all wet with dew,
And purple-misted in the fading light.
And joy I knew and sorrow at thy voice,
And the superb magnificence of love,--
The loneliness that saddens solitude,   10
And the sweet speech that makes it durable,--
The bitter longing and the keen desire,
The sweet companionship through quiet days
In the slow ample beauty of the world,
And the unutterable glad release   15

Within the temple of the holy night.
O Atthis, how I loved thee long ago
In that fair perished summer by the sea!

XXIV

I shall be ever maiden,
If thou be not my lover,
And no man shall possess me
Henceforth and forever.

But thou alone shalt gather   5
This fragile flower of beauty,--
To crush and keep the fragrance
Like a holy incense.

Thou only shalt remember
This love of mine, or hallow 10
The coming years with gladness,
Calm and pride and passion.

XXV

It was summer when I found you
In the meadow long ago,--

And the golden vetch was growing
  By the shore.

Did we falter when love took us   5
With a gust of great desire?
Does the barley bid the wind wait
  In his course?

XXVI

I recall thy white gown, cinctured
With a linen belt, whereon
Violets were wrought, and scented
With strange perfumes out of Egypt.

And I know thy foot was covered   5
With fair Lydian broidered straps;
And the petals from a rose-tree
Fell within the marble basin.

XXVII

Lover, art thou of a surety
Not a learner of the wood-god?
Has the madness of his music

Never touched thee?

Ah, thou dear and godlike mortal,   5
If Pan takes thee for his pupil,
Make me but another Syrinx
  For that piping.

XXVIII

With your head thrown backward
In my arm's safe hollow,
And your face all rosy
With the mounting fervour;

While the grave eyes greaten   5
With the wise new wonder,
Swimming in a love-mist
Like the haze of Autumn;

From that throat, the throbbing
Nightingale's for pleading,   10
Wayward, soft, and welling
Inarticulate love-notes,

Come the words that bubble
Up through broken laughter,
Sweeter than spring-water,   15
"Gods, I am so happy!"

XXIX

Ah, what am I but a torrent,
Headstrong, impetuous, broken,
Like the spent clamour of waters
  In the blue canyon?

Ah, what art thou but a fern-frond, 5
Wet with blown spray from the river,
Diffident, lovely, sequestered,
  Frail on the rock-ledge?

Yet, are we not for one brief day,
While the sun sleeps on the mountain,   10
Wild-hearted lover and loved one,
  Safe in Pan's keeping?

XXX

Love shakes my soul, like a mountain wind
  Falling upon the trees,
When they are swayed and whitened and bowed
  As the great gusts will.

I know why Daphne sped through the grove   5

When the bright god came by,
And shut herself in the laurel's heart
    For her silent doom.

Love fills my heart, like my lover's breath
    Filling the hollow flute,   10
Till the magic wood awakes and cries
    With remembrance and joy.

Ah, timid Syrinx, do I not know
    Thy tremor of sweet fear?
For a beautiful and imperious player   15
    Is the lord of life.

XXXI

Love, let the wind cry
On the dark mountain,
Bending the ash-trees
And the tall hemlocks,
With the great voice of   5
Thunderous legions,
How I adore thee.

Let the hoarse torrent
In the blue canyon,
Murmuring mightily 10
Out of the grey mist
Of primal chaos,

Cease not proclaiming
How I adore thee.

Let the long rhythm 15
Of crunching rollers,
Breaking and bellowing
On the white seaboard,
Titan and tireless,
Tell, while the world stands, 20
How I adore thee.

Love, let the clear call
Of the tree-cricket,
Frailest of creatures,
Green as the young grass,   25
Mark with his trilling
Resonant bell-note,
How I adore thee.

Let the glad lark-song
Over the meadow,   30
That melting lyric
Of molten silver,
Be for a signal
To listening mortals,
How I adore thee.   35

But more than all sounds,
Surer, serener,
Fuller with passion
And exultation,
Let the hushed whisper   40
In thine own heart say,

How I adore thee.

XXXII

Heart of mine, if all the altars
Of the ages stood before me,
Not one pure enough nor sacred
Could I find to lay this white, white
  Rose of love upon. 5

I who am not great enough to
Love thee with this mortal body
So impassionate with ardour,
But oh, not too small to worship
  While the sun shall shine,--   10

I would build a fragrant temple
To thee, in the dark green forest,
Of red cedar and fine sandal,
And there love thee with sweet service
  All my whole life long.   15

I would freshen it with flowers,
And the piney hill-wind through it
Should be sweetened with soft fervours
Of small prayers in gentle language
  Thou wouldst smile to hear.   20

And a tinkling Eastern wind-bell,

With its fluttering inscription,
From the rafters with bronze music
Should retard the quiet fleeting
  Of uncounted hours.   25

And my hero, while so human,
Should be even as the gods are,
In that shrine of utter gladness,
With the tranquil stars above it
  And the sea below. 30

XXXIII

Never yet, love, in earth's lifetime,
Hath any cunningest minstrel
Told the one seventh of wisdom,
Ravishment, ecstasy, transport,
Hid in the hue of the hyacinth's   5
  Purple in springtime.

Not in the lyre of Orpheus,
Not in the songs of Musaeus,
Lurked the unfathomed bewitchment
Wrought by the wind in the grasses,   10
Held by the rote of the sea-surf,
  In early summer.

Only to exquisite lovers,
Fashioned for beauty's fulfilment,
Mated as rhythm to reed-stop   15

Whence the wild music is moulded,
Ever appears the full measure
  Of the world's wonder.

XXXIV

"Who was Atthis?" men shall ask,
When the world is old, and time
Has accomplished without haste
The strange destiny of men.

Haply in that far-off age   5
One shall find these silver songs,
With their human freight, and guess
What a lover Sappho was.

XXXV

When the great pink mallow
Blossoms in the marshland,
Full of lazy summer
And soft hours,

Then I hear the summons   5
Not a mortal lover

Ever yet resisted,
Strange and far.

In the faint blue foothills,
Making magic music, 10
Pan is at his love-work
On the reeds.

I can guess the heart-stop,
Fall and lull and sequence,
Full of grief for Syrinx   15
Long ago.

Then the crowding madness,
Wild and keen and tender,
Trembles with the burden
Of great joy.   20

Nay, but well I follow,
All unskilled, that fluting.
Never yet was reed-nymph
Like to thee.

XXXVI

When I pass thy door at night
I a benediction breathe:
"Ye who have the sleeping world
  In your care,

"Guard the linen sweet and cool,   5
Where a lovely golden head
With its dreams of mortal bliss
  Slumbers now!"

XXXVII

Well I found you in the twilit garden,
Laid a lover's hand upon your shoulder,
And we both were made aware of loving
Past the reach of reason to unravel,
Or the much desiring heart to follow.   5

There we heard the breath among the grasses
And the gurgle of soft-running water,
Well contented with the spacious starlight,
The cool wind's touch and the deep blue distance,
Till the dawn came in with golden sandals. 10

XXXVIII

Will not men remember us
In the days to come hereafter,--
Thy warm-coloured loving beauty

And my love for thee?

Thou, the hyacinth that grows   5
By a quiet-running river;
I, the watery reflection
  And the broken gleam.

XXXIX

I grow weary of the foreign cities,
The sea travel and the stranger peoples.
Even the clear voice of hardy fortune
Dares me not as once on brave adventure.

For the heart of man must seek and wander,   5
Ask and question and discover knowledge;
Yet above all goodly things is wisdom,
And love greater than all understanding.

So, a mariner, I long for land-fall,--
When a darker purple on the sea-rim,   10
O'er the prow uplifted, shall be Lesbos
And the gleaming towers of Mitylene.

XL

Ah, what detains thee, Phaon,
So long from Mitylene,
Where now thy restless lover
Wearies for thy coming?

A fever burns me, Phaon;   5
My knees quake on the threshold,
And all my strength is loosened,
Slack with disappointment.

But thou wilt come, my Phaon,
Back from the sea like morning,   10
To quench in golden gladness
The ache of parted lovers.

XLI

Phaon, O my lover,
What should so detain thee,

Now the wind comes walking
Through the leafy twilight?

All the plum-leaves quiver   5
With the coolth and darkness,

After their long patience
In consuming ardour.

And the moving grasses
Have relief; the dew-drench 10

Comes to quell the parching
Ache of noon they suffered.

I alone of all things
Fret with unsluiced fire.

And there is no quenching   15
In the night for Sappho,

Since her lover Phaon
Leaves her unrequited.

XLII

O heart of insatiable longing,
What spell, what enchantment allures thee
Over the rim of the world
With the sails of the sea-going ships?

And when the rose-petals are scattered   5
At dead of still noon on the grass-plot,
What means this passionate grief,--

This infinite ache of regret?

XLIII

Surely somehow, in some measure,
There will be joy and fulfilment,--
Cease from this throb of desire,--
  Even for Sappho!

Surely some fortunate hour 5
Phaon will come, and his beauty
Be spent like water to plenish
  Need of that beauty!

Where is the breath of Poseidon,
Cool from the sea-floor with evening?   10
Why are Selene's white horses
  So long arriving?

XLIV

O but my delicate lover,
Is she not fair as the moonlight?
Is she not supple and strong
  For hurried passion?

Has not the god of the green world, 5
In his large tolerant wisdom,
Filled with the ardours of earth
  Her twenty summers?

Well did he make her for loving;
Well did he mould her for beauty; 10
Gave her the wish that is brave
  With understanding.

"O Pan, avert from this maiden
Sorrow, misfortune, bereavement,
Harm, and unhappy regret," 15
  Prays one fond mortal.

XLV

Softer than the hill-fog to the forest
Are the loving hands of my dear lover,
When she sleeps beside me in the starlight
And her beauty drenches me with rest.

As the quiet mist enfolds the beech-trees, 5
Even as she dreams her arms enfold me,
Half awaking with a hundred kisses
On the scarlet lily of her mouth.

XLVI

I seek and desire,
Even as the wind
That travels the plain
And stirs in the bloom
Of the apple-tree.   5

I wander through life,
With the searching mind
That is never at rest,
Till I reach the shade
Of my lover's door.   10

XLVII

Like torn sea-kelp in the drift
Of the great tides of the sea,
Carried past the harbour-mouth
To the deep beyond return,

I am buoyed and borne away   5
On the loveliness of earth,
Little caring, save for thee,
Past the portals of the night.

XLVIII

Fine woven purple linen
I bring thee from Phocaea,
That, beauty upon beauty,
A precious gift may cover
The lap where I have lain.   5

And a gold comb, and girdle,
And trinkets of white silver,
And gems are in my sea-chest,
Lest poor and empty-handed
Thy lover should return.   10

And I have brought from Tyre
A Pan-flute stained vermilion,
Wherein the gods have hidden
Love and desire and longing,
Which I shall loose for thee. 15

XLIX

When I am home from travel,
My eager foot will stay not
Until I reach the threshold

Where I went forth from thee.

And there, as darkness gathers   5
In the rose-scented garden,
The god who prospers music
Shall give me skill to play.

And thou shalt hear, all startled,
A flute blown in the twilight,   10
With the soft pleading magic
The green wood heard of old.

Then, lamp in hand, thy beauty
In the rose-marble entry!
And unreluctant Hermes   15
Shall give me words to say.

L

When I behold the pharos shine
And lay a path along the sea,
How gladly I shall feel the spray,
Standing upon the swinging prow;

And question of my pilot old,   5
How many watery leagues to sail
Ere we shall round the harbour reef
And anchor off the wharves of home!

LI

Is the day long,
O Lesbian maiden,
And the night endless
In thy lone chamber
In Mitylene?   5

All the bright day,
Until welcome evening
When the stars kindle
Over the harbour,
What tasks employ thee?   10

Passing the fountain
At golden sundown,
One of the home-going
Traffickers, hast thou
Thought of thy lover?   15

Nay, but how far
Too brief will the night be,
When I returning
To the dear portal
Hear my own heart beat!   20

LII

Lo, on the distance a dark blue ravine,
A fold in the mountainous forests of fir,
Cleft from the sky-line sheer down to the shore!

Above are the clouds and the white, pealing gulls,
At its foot is the rough broken foam of the sea,   5
With ever anon the long deep muffled roar,--
A sigh from the fitful great heart of the world.

Then inland just where the small meadow begins,
Well bulwarked with boulders that jut in the tide,
Lies safe beyond storm-beat the harbour in sun.   10

See where the black fishing-boats, each at its buoy,
Ride up on the swell with their dare-danger prows,
To sight o'er the sea-rim what venture may come!

And look, where the narrow white streets of the town
Leap up from the blue water's edge to the wood,   15
Scant room for man's range between mountain and sea,
And the market where woodsmen from over the hill
May traffic, and sailors from far foreign ports
With treasure brought in from the ends of the earth.

And see the third house on the left, with that gleam   20
Of red burnished copper--the hinge of the door
Whereat I shall enter, expected so oft
(Let love be your sea-star!), to voyage no more.

LIII

Art thou the top-most apple
The gatherers could not reach,
Reddening on the bough?
  Shall not I take thee?

Art thou a hyacinth blossom 5
The shepherds upon the hills
Have trodden into the ground?
  Shall not I lift thee?

Free is the young god Eros,
Paying no tribute to power, 10
Seeing no evil in beauty,
  Full of compassion.

Once having found the beloved,
However sorry or woeful,
However scornful of loving, 15
  Little it matters.

LIV

How soon will all my lovely days be over,
And I no more be found beneath the sun,--

Neither beside the many-murmuring sea,
Nor where the plain-winds whisper to the reeds,
Nor in the tall beech-woods among the hills   5
Where roam the bright-lipped Oreads, nor along
The pasture-sides where berry-pickers stray
And harmless shepherds pipe their sheep to fold!

For I am eager, and the flame of life
Burns quickly in the fragile lamp of clay.   10
Passion and love and longing and hot tears
Consume this mortal Sappho, and too soon
A great wind from the dark will blow upon me,
And I be no more found in the fair world,
For all the search of the revolving moon   15
And patient shine of everlasting stars.

LV

Soul of sorrow, why this weeping?
What immortal grief hath touched thee
With the poignancy of sadness,--
   Testament of tears?

Have the high gods deigned to show thee   5
Destiny, and disillusion
Fills thy heart at all things human,
   Fleeting and desired?

Nay, the gods themselves are fettered

By one law which links together   10
Truth and nobleness and beauty,
  Man and stars and sea.

And they only shall find freedom
Who with courage rise and follow
Where love leads beyond all peril,   15
  Wise beyond all words.

LVI

It never can be mine
To sit in the door in the sun
And watch the world go by,
A pageant and a dream;

For I was born for love,   5
And fashioned for desire,
Beauty, passion, and joy,
And sorrow and unrest;

And with all things of earth
Eternally must go,   10
Daring the perilous bourn
Of joyance and of death,

A strain of song by night,
A shadow on the hill,
A hint of odorous grass,   15

A murmur of the sea.

LVII

Others shall behold the sun
Through the long uncounted years,--
Not a maid in after time
  Wise as thou!

For the gods have given thee
Their best gift, an equal mind   5
That can only love, be glad,
  And fear not.

LVIII

Let thy strong spirit never fear,
Nor in thy virgin soul be thou afraid.
The gods themselves and the almightier fates
Cannot avail to harm

With outward and misfortunate chance   5
The radiant unshaken mind of him
Who at his being's centre will abide,
Secure from doubt and fear.

His wise and patient heart shall share
The strong sweet loveliness of all things made,   10
And the serenity of inward joy
Beyond the storm of tears.

LIX

Will none say of Sappho,
Speaking of her lovers,
And the love they gave her,--
Joy and days and beauty,
Flute-playing and roses,   5
Song and wine and laughter,--

Will none, musing, murmur,
"Yet, for all the roses,
All the flutes and lovers,
Doubt not she was lonely   10
As the sea, whose cadence
Haunts the world for ever."

LX

When I have departed,

Say but this behind me,
"Love was all her wisdom,
  All her care.

"Well she kept love's secret,--   5
Dared and never faltered,--
Laughed and never doubted
  Love would win.

"Let the world's rough triumph
Trample by above her,   10
She is safe forever
  From all harm.

"In a land that knows not
Bitterness nor sorrow,
She has found out all 15
  Of truth at last."

LXI

There is no more to say now thou art still,
There is no more to do now thou art dead,
There is no more to know now thy clear mind
Is back returned unto the gods who gave it.

Now thou art gone the use of life is past,   5
The meaning and the glory and the pride,
There is no joyous friend to share the day,

And on the threshold no awaited shadow.

LXII

Play up, play up thy silver flute;
The crickets all are brave;
Glad is the red autumnal earth
  And the blue sea.

Play up thy flawless silver flute;   5
Dead ripe are fruit and grain.
When love puts on his scarlet coat,
  Put off thy care.

LXIII

A beautiful child is mine,
Formed like a golden flower,
Cleis the loved one.
And above her I value
Not all the Lydian land,   5
Nor lovely Hellas.

LXIV

Ah, but now henceforth
Only one meaning
Has life for me.

Only one purport,
Measure and beauty, 5
Has the bright world.

What mean the wood-winds,
Colour and morning,
Bird, stream, and hill?

And the brave city   10
With its enchantment?
Thee, only thee!

LXV

Softly the wind moves through the radiant morning,
And the warm sunlight sinks into the valley,
Filling the green earth with a quiet joyance,
  Strength, and fulfilment.

Even so, gentle, strong and wise and happy,   5
Through the soul and substance of my being,

Comes the breath of thy great love to me-ward,
  O thou dear mortal.

LXVI

What the west wind whispers
At the end of summer,
When the barley harvest
Ripens to the sickle,
  Who can tell?   5

What means the fine music
Of the dry cicada,
Through the long noon hours
Of the autumn stillness,
  Who can say?   10

How the grape ungathered
With its bloom of blueness
Greatens on the trellis
Of the brick-walled garden,
  Who can know?   15

Yet I, too, am greatened,
Keep the note of gladness,
Travel by the wind's road,
Through this autumn leisure,--
  By thy love. 20

LXVII

Indoors the fire is kindled;
Beechwood is piled on the hearthstone;
Cold are the chattering oak-leaves;
And the ponds frost-bitten.

Softer than rainfall at twilight,   5
Bringing the fields benediction
And the hills quiet and greyness,
Are my long thoughts of thee.

How should thy friend fear the seasons?
They only perish of winter   10
Whom Love, audacious and tender,
Never hath visited.

LXVIII

You ask how love can keep the mortal soul
Strong to the pitch of joy throughout the years.

Ask how your brave cicada on the bough
Keeps the long sweet insistence of his cry;

Ask how the Pleiads steer across the night 5
In their serene unswerving mighty course;

Ask how the wood-flowers waken to the sun,
Unsummoned save by some mysterious word;

Ask how the wandering swallows find your eaves
Upon the rain-wind with returning spring; 10

Ask who commands the ever-punctual tide
To keep the pendulous rhythm of the sea;

And you shall know what leads the heart of man
To the far haven of his hopes and fears.

LXIX

Like a tall forest were their spears,
Their banners like a silken sea,
When the great host in splendour passed
Across the crimson sinking sun.

And then the bray of brazen horns 5
Arose above their clanking march,
As the long waving column filed
Into the odorous purple dusk.

O lover, in this radiant world
Whence is the race of mortal men, 10

So frail, so mighty, and so fond,
That fleets into the vast unknown?

LXX

My lover smiled, "O friend, ask not
The journey's end, nor whence we are.
That whistling boy who minds his goats
So idly in the grey ravine,

"The brown-backed rower drenched with spray,   5
The lemon-seller in the street,
And the young girl who keeps her first
Wild love-tryst at the rising moon,--

"Lo, these are wiser than the wise.
And not for all our questioning   10
Shall we discover more than joy,
Nor find a better thing than love!

"Let pass the banners and the spears,
The hate, the battle, and the greed;
For greater than all gifts is peace,   15
And strength is in the tranquil mind."

LXXI

Ye who have the stable world
In the keeping of your hands,
Flocks and men, the lasting hills,
And the ever-wheeling stars;

Ye who freight with wondrous things   5
The wide-wandering heart of man
And the galleon of the moon,
On those silent seas of foam;

Oh, if ever ye shall grant
Time and place and room enough   10
To this fond and fragile heart
Stifled with the throb of love,

On that day one grave-eyed Fate,
Pausing in her toil, shall say,
"Lo, one mortal has achieved   15
Immortality of love!"

LXXII

I heard the gods reply:
"Trust not the future with its perilous chance;
The fortunate hour is on the dial now.

"To-day be wise and great,
And put off hesitation and go forth 5
With cheerful courage for the diurnal need.

"Stout be the heart, nor slow
The foot to follow the impetuous will,
Nor the hand slack upon the loom of deeds.

"Then may the Fates look up   10
And smile a little in their tolerant way,
Being full of infinite regard for men."

LXXIII

The sun on the tide, the peach on the bough,
The blue smoke over the hill,
And the shadows trailing the valley-side,
Make up the autumn day.

Ah, no, not half! Thou art not here 5
Under the bronze beech-leaves,
And thy lover's soul like a lonely child
Roams through an empty room.

LXXIV

If death be good,
Why do the gods not die?
If life be ill,
Why do the gods still live?

If love be naught,   5
Why do the gods still love?
If love be all,
What should men do but love?

LXXV

Tell me what this life means,
O my prince and lover,
With the autumn sunlight
On thy bronze-gold head?

With thy clear voice sounding   5
Through the silver twilight,--
What is the lost secret
Of the tacit earth?

LXXVI

Ye have heard how Marsyas,
In the folly of his pride,
Boasted of a matchless skill,--
When the great god's back was turned;

How his fond imagining   5
Fell to ashes cold and grey,
When the flawless player came
In serenity and light.

So it was with those I loved
In the years ere I loved thee. 10
Many a saying sounds like truth,
Until Truth itself is heard.

Many a beauty only lives
Until Beauty passes by,
And the mortal is forgot   15
In the shadow of the god.

LXXVII

Hour by hour I sit,
Watching the silent door.
Shadows go by on the wall,

And steps in the street.

Expectation and doubt   5
Flutter my timorous heart.
So many hurrying home--
And thou still away.

LXXVIII

Once in the shining street,
In the heart of a seaboard town,
As I waited, behold, there came
The woman I loved.

As when, in the early spring,   5
A daffodil blooms in the grass,
Golden and gracious and glad,
The solitude smiled.

LXXIX

How strange is love, O my lover!
With what enchantment and power
Does it not come upon mortals,
Learned or heedless!

How far away and unreal,   5
Faint as blue isles in a sunset
Haze-golden, all else of life seems,
Since I have known thee!

LXXX

How to say I love you:
What, if I but live it,
Were the use in that, love?
  Small, indeed.

Only, every moment 5
Of this waking lifetime
Let me be your lover
  And your friend!

Ah, but then, as sure as
Blossom breaks from bud-sheath,   10
When along the hillside
  Spring returns,

Golden speech should flower
From the soul so cherished,
And the mouth your kisses   15
  Filled with fire.

LXXXI

Hark, love, to the tambourines
Of the minstrels in the street,
And one voice that throbs and soars
Clear above the clashing time!

Some Egyptian royal love-lilt,   5
Some Sidonian refrain,
Vows of Paphos or of Tyre,
Mount against the silver sun.

Pleading, piercing, yet serene,
Vagrant in a foreign town,   10
From what passion was it born,
In what lost land over sea?

LXXXII

Over the roofs the honey-coloured moon,
With purple shadows on the silver grass,

And the warm south-wind on the curving sea,
While we two, lovers past all turmoil now,

Watch from the window the white sails come in, 5

Bearing what unknown ventures safe to port!

So falls the hour of twilight and of love
With wizardry to loose the hearts of men,

And there is nothing more in this great world
Than thou and I, and the blue dome of dusk.   10

LXXXIII

In the quiet garden world,
Gold sunlight and shadow leaves
Flicker on the wall.

And the wind, a moment since,
With rose-petals strewed the path   5
And the open door.

Now the moon-white butterflies
Float across the liquid air,
Glad as in a dream;

And, across thy lover's heart,   10
Visions of one scarlet mouth
With its maddening smile.

LXXXIV

Soft was the wind in the beech-trees;
Low was the surf on the shore;
In the blue dusk one planet
Like a great sea-pharos shone.

But nothing to me were the sea-sounds,   5
The wind and the yellow star,
When over my breast the banner
Of your golden hair was spread.

LXXXV

Have you heard the news of Sappho's garden,
And the Golden Rose of Mitylene,
Which the bending brown-armed rowers lately
Brought from over sea, from lonely Pontus?

In a meadow by the river Halys,   5
Where some wood-god hath the world in keeping,
On a burning summer noon they found her,
Lovely as a Dryad, and more tender.

Her these eyes have seen, and not another
Shall behold, till time takes all things goodly,   10
So surpassing fair and fond and wondrous,--
Such a slave as, worth a great king's ransom,

No man yet of all the sons of mortals
But would lose his soul for and regret not;
So hath Beauty compassed all her children 15
With the cords of longing and desire.

Only Hermes, master of word music,
Ever yet in glory of gold language
Could ensphere the magical remembrance
Of her melting, half sad, wayward beauty, 20

Or devise the silver phrase to frame her,
The inevitable name to call her,
Half a sigh and half a kiss when whispered,
Like pure air that feeds a forge's hunger.

Not a painter in the Isles of Hellas   25
Could portray her, mix the golden tawny
With bright stain of poppies, or ensanguine
Like the life her darling mouth's vermilion,

So that, in the ages long hereafter,
When we shall be dust of perished summers,   30
Any man could say who found that likeness,
Smiling gently on it, "This was Gorgo!"

LXXXVI

Love is so strong a thing,

The very gods must yield,
When it is welded fast
With the unflinching truth.

Love is so frail a thing,   5
A word, a look, will kill.
Oh lovers, have a care
How ye do deal with love.

LXXXVII

Hadst thou, with all thy loveliness, been true,
Had I, with all my tenderness, been strong,
We had not made this ruin out of life,
This desolation in a world of joy,
  My poor Gorgo.   5

Yet even the high gods at times do err;
Be therefore thou not overcome with woe,
But dedicate anew to greater love
An equal heart, and be thy radiant self
  Once more, Gorgo. 10

LXXXVIII

As, on a morn, a traveller might emerge
From the deep green seclusion of the hills,
By a cool road through forest and through fern,
Little frequented, winding, followed long
With joyous expectation and day-dreams, 5
And on a sudden, turning a great rock
Covered with frondage, dark with dripping water,
Behold the seaboard full of surf and sound,
With all the space and glory of the world
Above the burnished silver of the sea,--   10

Even so it was upon that first spring day
When time, that is a devious path for men,
Led me all lonely to thy door at last;
And all thy splendid beauty, gracious and glad,
(Glad as bright colour, free as wind or air, 15
And lovelier than racing seas of foam)
Bore sense and soul and mind at once away
To a pure region where the gods might dwell,
Making of me, a vagrant child before,
A servant of joy at Aphrodite's will. 20

LXXXIX

Where shall I look for thee,

Where find thee now,
O my lost Atthis?

Storm bars the harbour,
And snow keeps the pass   5
In the blue mountains.

Bitter the wind whistles,
Pale is the sun,
And the days shorten.

Close to the hearthstone,   10
With long thoughts of thee,
Thy lonely lover

Sits now, remembering
All the spent hours
And thy fair beauty.   15

Ah, when the hyacinth
Wakens with spring,
And buds the laurel,

Doubt not, some morning
When all earth revives,   20
Hearing Pan's flute-call

Over the river-beds,
Over the hills,
Sounding the summons,

I shall look up and behold   25
In the door,

Smiling, expectant,

Loving as ever
And glad as of old,
My own lost Atthis!   30

XC

A sad, sad face, and saddest eyes that ever
  Beheld the sun,
Whence came the grief that makes of all thy beauty
  One sad sweet smile?

In this bright portrait, where the painter fixed them,   5
  I still behold
The eyes that gladdened, and the lips that loved me,
  And, gold on rose,

The cloud of hair that settles on one shoulder
  Slipped from its vest.   10
I almost hear thy Mitylenean love-song
  In the spring night,

When the still air was odorous with blossoms,
  And in the hour
Thy first wild girl's-love trembled into being,   15
  Glad, glad and fond.

Ah, where is all that wonder? What god's malice

Undid that joy
And set the seal of patient woe upon thee,
  O my lost love?   20

XCI

Why have the gods in derision
Severed us, heart of my being?
Where have they lured thee to wander,
  O my lost lover?

While now I sojourn with sorrow, 5
Having remorse for my comrade,
What town is blessed with thy beauty,
  Gladdened and prospered?

Nay, who could love as I loved thee,
With whom thy beauty was mingled   10
In those spring days when the swallows
  Came with the south wind?

Then I became as that shepherd
Loved by Selene on Latmus,
Once when her own summer magic 15
  Took hold upon her

With a sweet madness, and thenceforth
Her mortal lover must wander
Over the wide world for ever,

Like one enchanted.20

XCII

Like a red lily in the meadow grasses,
Swayed by the wind and burning in the sunlight,
I saw you, where the city chokes with traffic,
Bearing among the passers-by your beauty,
Unsullied, wild, and delicate as a flower.   5
And then I knew, past doubt or peradventure,
Our loved and mighty Eleusinian mother
Had taken thought of me for her pure worship,
And of her favour had assigned my comrade
For the Great Mysteries,--knew I should find you 10
When the dusk murmured with its new-made lovers,
And we be no more foolish but wise children,
And well content partake of joy together,
As she ordains and human hearts desire.

XCIII

When in the spring the swallows all return,
And the bleak bitter sea grows mild once more,
With all its thunders softened to a sigh;

When to the meadows the young green comes back,
And swelling buds put forth on every bough,   5
With wild-wood odours on the delicate air;

Ah, then, in that so lovely earth wilt thou
With all thy beauty love me all one way,
And make me all thy lover as before?

Lo, where the white-maned horses of the surge,   10
Plunging in thunderous onset to the shore,
Trample and break and charge along the sand!

XCIV

Cold is the wind where Daphne sleeps,
That was so tender and so warm
With loving,--with a loveliness
Than her own laurel lovelier.

Now pipes the bitter wind for her, 5
And the snow sifts about her door,
While far below her frosty hill
The racing billows plunge and boom.

XCV

Hark, where Poseidon's
White racing horses
Trample with tumult
The shelving seaboard!

Older than Saturn,   5
Older than Rhea,
That mournful music,
Falling and surging

With the vast rhythm
Ceaseless, eternal,   10
Keeps the long tally
Of all things mortal.

How many lovers
Hath not its lulling
Cradled to slumber
With the ripe flowers,   15

Ere for our pleasure
This golden summer
Walked through the corn-lands
In gracious splendour!   20

How many loved ones
Will it not croon to,
In the long spring-days
Through coming ages,

When all our day-dreams   25
Have been forgotten,
And none remembers
Even thy beauty!

They too shall slumber
In quiet places,   30
And mighty sea-sounds
Call them unheeded.

XCVI

Hark, my lover, it is spring!
On the wind a faint far call
Wakes a pang within my heart,
Unmistakable and keen.

At the harbour mouth a sail **5**
Glimmers in the morning sun,
And the ripples at her prow
Whiten into crumbling foam,

As she forges outward bound
For the teeming foreign ports.   **10**
Through the open window now,
Hear the sailors lift a song!

In the meadow ground the frogs

With their deafening flutes begin,--
The old madness of the world   15
In their golden throats again.

Little fifers of live bronze,
Who hath taught you with wise lore
To unloose the strains of joy,
When Orion seeks the west?20

And you feathered flute-players,
Who instructed you to fill
All the blossomy orchards now
With melodious desire?

I doubt not our father Pan   25
Hath a care of all these things.
In some valley of the hills
Far away and misty-blue,

By quick water he hath cut
A new pipe, and set the wood   30
To his smiling lips, and blown,
That earth's rapture be restored.

And those wild Pandean stops
Mark the cadence life must keep.
O my lover, be thou glad;   35
It is spring in Hellas now.

XCVII

When the early soft spring wind comes blowing
Over Rhodes and Samos and Miletus,
From the seven mouths of Nile to Lesbos,
Freighted with sea-odours and gold sunshine,

What news spreads among the island people   5
In the market-place of Mitylene,
Lending that unwonted stir of gladness
To the busy streets and thronging doorways?

Is it word from Ninus or Arbela,
Babylon the great, or Northern Imbros?   10
Have the laden galleons been sighted
Stoutly labouring up the sea from Tyre?

Nay, 'tis older news that foreign sailor
With the cheek of sea-tan stops to prattle
To the young fig-seller with her basket   15
And the breasts that bud beneath her tunic,

And I hear it in the rustling tree-tops.
All this passionate bright tender body
Quivers like a leaf the wind has shaken,
Now love wanders through the aisles of springtime.   20

XCVIII

I am more tremulous than shaken reeds,
And love has made me like the river water.

Thy voice is as the hill-wind over me,
And all my changing heart gives heed, my lover.

Before thy least lost murmur I must sigh,   5
Or gladden with thee as the sun-path glitters.

XCIX

Over the wheat-field,
Over the hill-crest,
Swoops and is gone
The beat of a wild wing,
Brushing the pine-tops,   5
Bending the poppies,
Hurrying Northward
With golden summer.

What premonition,
O purple swallow,   10
Told thee the happy
Hour of migration?

Hark! On the threshold
(Hush, flurried heart in me!),
Was there a footfall? 15
Did no one enter?

Soon will a shepherd
In rugged Dacia,
Folding his gentle
Ewes in the twilight, 20
Lifting a level
Gaze from the sheepfold,
Say to his fellows,
"Lo, it is springtime."

This very hour   25
In Mitylene,
Will not a young girl
Say to her lover,
Lifting her moon-white
Arms to enlace him,   30
Ere the glad sigh comes,
"Lo, it is lovetime!"

C

Once more the rain on the mountain,
Once more the wind in the valley,
With the soft odours of springtime
And the long breath of remembrance,

O Lityerses! 5

Warm is the sun in the city.
On the street corners with laughter
Traffic the flower-girls. Beauty
Blossoms once more for thy pleasure
  In many places.   10

Gentlier now falls the twilight,
With the slim moon in the pear-trees;
And the green frogs in the meadows
Blow on shrill pipes to awaken
  Thee, Lityerses.   15

Gladlier now crimson morning
Flushes fair-built Mitylene,--
Portico, temple, and column,--
Where the young garlanded women
Praise thee with singing.   20

Ah, but what burden of sorrow
Tinges their slow stately chorus,
Though spring revisits the glad earth?
Wilt thou not wake to their summons,
  O Lityerses? 25

Shall they then never behold thee,--
Nevermore see thee returning
Down the blue cleft of the mountains,
Nor in the purple of evening
  Welcome thy coming?   30

Nevermore answer thy glowing

Youth with their ardour, nor cherish
With lovely longing thy spirit,
Nor with soft laughter beguile thee,
  O Lityerses? 35

Heedless, assuaged, art thou sleeping
Where the spring sun cannot find thee,
Nor the wind waken, nor woodlands
Bloom for thy innocent rapture
Through golden hours?   40

Hast thou no passion nor pity
For thy deserted companions?
Never again will thy beauty
Quell their desire nor rekindle,
  O Lityerses? 45

Nay, but in vain their clear voices
Call thee. Thy sensitive beauty
Is become part of the fleeting
Loveliness, merged in the pathos
  Of all things mortal.50

In the faint fragrance of flowers,
On the sweet draft of the sea-wind,
Linger strange hints now that loosen
Tears for thy gay gentle spirit,
  O Lityerses! 55

EPILOGUE

Now the hundred songs are made,
And the pause comes. Loving Heart,
There must be an end to summer,
And the flute be laid aside.

On a day the frost will come,   5
Walking through the autumn world,
Hushing all the brave endeavour
Of the crickets in the grass.

On a day (Oh, far from now!)
Earth will hear this voice no more; 10
For it shall be with thy lover
As with Linus long ago.

All the happy songs he wrought
From remembrance soon must fade,
As the wash of silver moonlight   15
From a purple-dark ravine.

Frail as dew upon the grass
Or the spindrift of the sea,
Out of nothing they were fashioned
And to nothing must return. 20

Nay, but something of thy love,
Passion, tenderness, and joy,
Some strange magic of thy beauty,
Some sweet pathos of thy tears,

Must imperishably cling   25
To the cadence of the words,
Like a spell of lost enchantments
Laid upon the hearts of men.

Wild and fleeting as the notes
Blown upon a woodland pipe,   30
They must haunt the earth with gladness
And a tinge of old regret.

For the transport in their rhythm
Was the throb of thy desire,
And thy lyric moods shall quicken 35
Souls of lovers yet unborn.

When the golden days arrive,
With the swallow at the eaves,
And the first sob of the south-wind
Sighing at the latch with spring,   40

Long hereafter shall thy name
Be recalled through foreign lands,
And thou be a part of sorrow
When the Linus songs are sung.

The Codes Of Hammurabi And Moses
W. W. Davies

QTY

The discovery of the Hammurabi Code is one of the greatest achievements of archaeology, and is of paramount interest, not only to the student of the Bible, but also to all those interested in ancient history...

Religion   **ISBN:** *1-59462-338-4*

Pages:132
MSRP $12.95

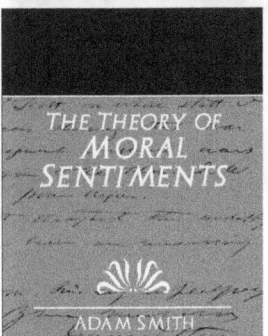

The Theory of Moral Sentiments
Adam Smith

QTY

This work from 1749. contains original theories of conscience amd moral judgment and it is the foundation for systemof morals.

Philosophy **ISBN:** *1-59462-777-0*

Pages:536
MSRP $19.95

Jessica's First Prayer
Hesba Stretton

QTY

In a screened and secluded corner of one of the many railway-bridges which span the streets of London there could be seen a few years ago, from five o'clock every morning until half past eight, a tidily set-out coffee-stall, consisting of a trestle and board, upon which stood two large tin cans, with a small fire of charcoal burning under each so as to keep the coffee boiling during the early hours of the morning when the work-people were thronging into the city on their way to their daily toil...

Childrens   **ISBN:** *1-59462-373-2*

Pages:84
MSRP $9.95

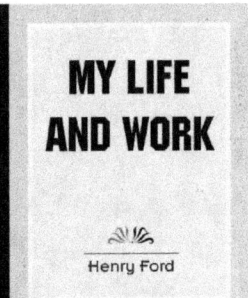

My Life and Work
Henry Ford

QTY

Henry Ford revolutionized the world with his implementation of mass production for the Model T automobile. Gain valuable business insight into his life and work with his own auto-biography... "We have only started on our development of our country we have not as yet, with all our talk of wonderful progress, done more than scratch the surface. The progress has been wonderful enough but..."

Biographies/   **ISBN:** *1-59462-198-5*

Pages:300
MSRP $21.95

The Art of Cross-Examination
Francis Wellman

QTY

I presume it is the experience of every author, after his first book is published upon an important subject, to be almost overwhelmed with a wealth of ideas and illustrations which could readily have been included in his book, and which to his own mind, at least, seem to make a second edition inevitable. Such certainly was the case with me; and when the first edition had reached its sixth impression in five months, I rejoiced to learn that it seemed to my publishers that the book had met with a sufficiently favorable reception to justify a second and considerably enlarged edition. ..

Pages:412

Reference   **ISBN:** *1-59462-647-2*   *MSRP $19.95*

On the Duty of Civil Disobedience
Henry David Thoreau

QTY

Thoreau wrote his famous essay, On the Duty of Civil Disobedience, as a protest against an unjust but popular war and the immoral but popular institution of slave-owning. He did more than write—he declined to pay his taxes, and was hauled off to gaol in consequence. Who can say how much this refusal of his hastened the end of the war and of slavery ?

Law   **ISBN:** *1-59462-747-9*   **Pages:48**

MSRP $7.45

Dream Psychology Psychoanalysis for Beginners
Sigmund Freud

QTY

Sigmund Freud, born Sigismund Schlomo Freud (May 6, 1856 - September 23, 1939), was a Jewish-Austrian neurologist and psychiatrist who co-founded the psychoanalytic school of psychology. Freud is best known for his theories of the unconscious mind, especially involving the mechanism of repression; his redefinition of sexual desire as mobile and directed towards a wide variety of objects; and his therapeutic techniques, especially his understanding of transference in the therapeutic relationship and the presumed value of dreams as sources of insight into unconscious desires.

Pages:196

Psychology   **ISBN:** *1-59462-905-6*   *MSRP $15.45*

The Miracle of Right Thought
Orison Swett Marden

QTY

Believe with all of your heart that you will do what you were made to do. When the mind has once formed the habit of holding cheerful, happy, prosperous pictures, it will not be easy to form the opposite habit. It does not matter how improbable or how far away this realization may see, or how dark the prospects may be, if we visualize them as best we can, as vividly as possible, hold tenaciously to them and vigorously struggle to attain them, they will gradually become actualized, realized in the life. But a desire, a longing without endeavor, a yearning abandoned or held indifferently will vanish without realization.

Pages:360

Self Help   **ISBN:** *1-59462-644-8*   *MSRP $25.45*

QTY

☐ **The Rosicrucian Cosmo-Conception Mystic Christianity** *by Max Heindel*   ISBN: *1-59462-188-8* **$38.95**
The Rosicrucian Cosmo-conception is not dogmatic, neither does it appeal to any other authority than the reason of the student. It is: not controversial, but is: sent forth in the, hope that it may help to clear...   New Age/Religion Pages 646

☐ **Abandonment To Divine Providence** *by Jean-Pierre de Caussade*   ISBN: *1-59462-228-0* **$25.95**
"The Rev. Jean Pierre de Caussade was one of the most remarkable spiritual writers of the Society of Jesus in France in the 18th Century. His death took place at Toulouse in 1751. His works have gone through many editions and have been republished...   Inspirational/Religion Pages 400

☐ **Mental Chemistry** *by Charles Haanel*   ISBN: *1-59462-192-6* **$23.95**
Mental Chemistry allows the change of material conditions by combining and appropriately utilizing the power of the mind. Much like applied chemistry creates something new and unique out of careful combinations of chemicals the mastery of mental chemistry...   New Age Pages 354

☐ **The Letters of Robert Browning and Elizabeth Barret Barrett 1845-1846 vol II**   ISBN: *1-59462-193-4* **$35.95**
by Robert Browning and Elizabeth Barrett   Biographies Pages 596

☐ **Gleanings In Genesis (volume I)** *by Arthur W. Pink*   ISBN: *1-59462-130-6* **$27.45**
Appropriately has Genesis been termed "the seed plot of the Bible" for in it we have, in germ form, almost all of the great doctrines which are afterwards fully developed in the books of Scripture which follow...   Religion/Inspirational Pages 420

☐ **The Master Key** *by L. W. de Laurence*   ISBN: *1-59462-001-6* **$30.95**
In no branch of human knowledge has there been a more lively increase of the spirit of research during the past few years than in the study of Psychology, Concentration and Mental Discipline. The requests for authentic lessons in Thought Control, Mental Discipline and...   New Age/Business Pages 422

☐ **The Lesser Key Of Solomon Goetia** *by L. W. de Laurence*   ISBN: *1-59462-092-X* **$9.95**
This translation of the first book of the "Lernegton" which is now for the first time made accessible to students of Talismanic Magic was done, after careful collation and edition, from numerous Ancient Manuscripts in Hebrew, Latin, and French...   New Age/Occult Pages 92

☐ **Rubaiyat Of Omar Khayyam** *by Edward Fitzgerald*   ISBN:*1-59462-332-5* **$13.95**
Edward Fitzgerald, whom the world has already learned, in spite of his own efforts to remain within the shadow of anonymity, to look upon as one of the rarest poets of the century, was born at Bredfield, in Suffolk, on the 31st of March, 1809. He was the third son of John Purcell...   Music Pages 172

☐ **Ancient Law** *by Henry Maine*   ISBN: *1-59462-128-4* **$29.95**
The chief object of the following pages is to indicate some of the earliest ideas of mankind, as they are reflected in Ancient Law, and to point out the relation of those ideas to modern thought.   Religion/History Pages 452

☐ **Far-Away Stories** *by William J. Locke*   ISBN: *1-59462-129-2* **$19.45**
"Good wine needs no bush, but a collection of mixed vintages does. And this book is just such a collection. Some of the stories I do not want to remain buried for ever in the museum files of dead magazine-numbers an author's not unpardonable vanity..."   Fiction Pages 272

☐ **Life of David Crockett** *by David Crockett*   ISBN: *1-59462-250-7* **$27.45**
"Colonel David Crockett was one of the most remarkable men of the times in which he lived. Born in humble life, but gifted with a strong will, an indomitable courage, and unremitting perseverance...   Biographies/New Age Pages 424

☐ **Lip-Reading** *by Edward Nitchie*   ISBN: *1-59462-206-X* **$25.95**
Edward B. Nitchie, founder of the New York School for the Hard of Hearing, now the Nitchie School of Lip-Reading, Inc, wrote "LIP-READING Principles and Practice". The development and perfecting of this meritorious work on lip-reading was an undertaking...   How-to Pages 400

☐ **A Handbook of Suggestive Therapeutics, Applied Hypnotism, Psychic Science**   ISBN: *1-59462-214-0* **$24.95**
by Henry Munro   Health/New Age/Health/Self-help Pages 376

☐ **A Doll's House: and Two Other Plays** *by Henrik Ibsen*   ISBN: *1-59462-112-8* **$19.95**
Henrik Ibsen created this classic when in revolutionary 1848 Rome. Introducing some striking concepts in playwriting for the realist genre, this play has been studied the world over.   Fiction/Classics/Plays 308

☐ **The Light of Asia** *by sir Edwin Arnold*   ISBN: *1-59462-204-3* **$13.95**
In this poetic masterpiece, Edwin Arnold describes the life and teachings of Buddha. The man who was to become known as Buddha to the world was born as Prince Gautama of India but he rejected the worldly riches and abandoned the reigns of power when...   Religion/History/Biographies Pages 170

☐ **The Complete Works of Guy de Maupassant** *by Guy de Maupassant*   ISBN: *1-59462-157-8* **$16.95**
"For days and days, nights and nights, I had dreamed of that first kiss which was to consecrate our engagement, and I knew not on what spot I should put my lips..."   Fiction/Classics Pages 240

☐ **The Art of Cross-Examination** *by Francis L. Wellman*   ISBN: *1-59462-309-0* **$26.95**
Written by a renowned trial lawyer, Wellman imparts his experience and uses case studies to explain how to use psychology to extract desired information through questioning.   How-to/Science/Reference Pages 408

☐ **Answered or Unanswered?** *by Louisa Vaughan*   ISBN: *1-59462-248-5* **$10.95**
Miracles of Faith in China   Religion Pages 112

☐ **The Edinburgh Lectures on Mental Science (1909)** *by Thomas*   ISBN: *1-59462-008-3* **$11.95**
This book contains the substance of a course of lectures recently given by the writer in the Queen Street Hail, Edinburgh. Its purpose is to indicate the Natural Principles governing the relation between Mental Action and Material Conditions...   New Age/Psychology Pages 148

☐ **Ayesha** *by H. Rider Haggard*   ISBN: *1-59462-301-5* **$24.95**
Verily and indeed it is the unexpected that happens! Probably if there was one person upon the earth from whom the Editor of this, and of a certain previous history, did not expect to hear again...   Classics Pages 380

☐ **Ayala's Angel** *by Anthony Trollope*   ISBN: *1-59462-352-X* **$29.95**
The two girls were both pretty, but Lucy who was twenty-one who supposed to be simple and comparatively unattractive, whereas Ayala was credited, as her Bombwhat romantic name might show, with poetic charm and a taste for romance. Ayala when her father died was nineteen...   Fiction Pages 484

☐ **The American Commonwealth** *by James Bryce*   ISBN: *1-59462-286-8* **$34.45**
An interpretation of American democratic political theory. It examines political mechanics and society from the perspective of Scotsman James Bryce   Politics Pages 572

☐ **Stories of the Pilgrims** *by Margaret P. Pumphrey*   ISBN: *1-59462-116-0* **$17.95**
This book explores pilgrims religious oppression in England as well as their escape to Holland and eventual crossing to America on the Mayflower, and their early days in New England...   History Pages 268

www.bookjungle.com *email: sales@bookjungle.com fax: 630-214-0564 mail: Book Jungle PO Box 2226 Champaign, IL 61825*

QTY

The Fasting Cure *by Sinclair Upton*   ISBN: *1-59462-222-1*   **$13.95**
*In the Cosmopolitan Magazine for May, 1910, and in the Contemporary Review (London) for April, 1910, I published an article dealing with my experi-
ences in fasting. I have written a great many magazine articles, but never one which attracted so much attention... New Age/Self Help/Health Pages 164*

Hebrew Astrology *by Sepharial*   ISBN: *1-59462-308-2*   **$13.45**
*In these days of advanced thinking it is a matter of common observation that we have left many of the old landmarks behind and that we are now pressing
forward to greater heights and to a wider horizon than that which represented the mind-content of our progenitors...   Astrology Pages 144*

Thought Vibration or The Law of Attraction in the Thought World   ISBN: *1-59462-127-6*   **$12.95**
by William Walker Atkinson   *Psychology/Religion Pages 144*

Optimism *by Helen Keller*   ISBN: *1-59462-108-X*   **$15.95**
*Helen Keller was blind, deaf, and mute since 19 months old, yet famously learned how to overcome these handicaps, communicate with the world, and
spread her lectures promoting optimism. An inspiring read for everyone...   Biographies/Inspirational Pages 84*

Sara Crewe *by Frances Burnett*   ISBN: *1-59462-360-0*   **$9.45**
*In the first place, Miss Minchin lived in London. Her home was a large, dull, tall one, in a large, dull square, where all the houses were alike, and all the
sparrows were alike, and where all the door-knockers made the same heavy sound...   Childrens/Classic Pages 88*

The Autobiography of Benjamin Franklin *by Benjamin Franklin*   ISBN: *1-59462-135-7*   **$24.95**
*The Autobiography of Benjamin Franklin has probably been more extensively read than any other American historical work, and no other book of its kind
has had such ups and downs of fortune. Franklin lived for many years in England, where he was agent...   Biographies/History Pages 332*

Name	
Email	
Telephone	
Address	
City, State ZIP	

☐ **Credit Card**   ☐ **Check / Money Order**

Credit Card Number	
Expiration Date	
Signature	

Please Mail to: Book Jungle
PO Box 2226
Champaign, IL 61825
or Fax to: 630-214-0564

ORDERING INFORMATION

web: *www.bookjungle.com*
email: *sales@bookjungle.com*
fax: *630-214-0564*
mail: *Book Jungle PO Box 2226 Champaign, IL 61825*
or PayPal *to sales@bookjungle.com*

Please contact us for bulk discounts

DIRECT-ORDER TERMS

**20% Discount if You Order
Two or More Books**
Free Domestic Shipping!
Accepted: Master Card, Visa,
Discover, American Express

www.ingramcontent.com/pod-product-compliance
Lightning Source LLC
Chambersburg PA
CBHW081158170626
46813CB00009B/3233